P9-DCM-882

WEEKLY READER
CHILDREN'S BOOK CLUB

WEEKLY READER CHILDREN'S BOOK CLUB *presents*

Gregory

Books by Robert Bright

The Friendly Bear
Georgie
Georgie and the Magician
Georgie and the Robbers
Georgie to the Rescue
Georgie's Halloween
Gregory
I Like Red
Me and the Bears
Richard Brown and the Dragon
Which Is Willy?

Gregory

THE NOISIEST AND STRONGEST BOY IN GRANGERS GROVE

by Robert Bright

Doubleday & Company, Inc., Garden City, New York

Library of Congress Catalog Card Number: 69-10718

Printed in the United States of America
Weekly Reader Children's Book Club Edition
Primary Division

For Kenny

Gregory could run faster than the fastest rabbit...

and jump higher than the highest haystack...

and holler so loud you had to hold your hat.

Gregory was the strongest and noisiest boy in Grangers Grove. And oh, was he proud of himself!

Now Gregory had a grandma who lived in a little house in the hollow, and she made the best griddle cakes in Grangers Grove. And oh, how Gregory loved Grandma's griddle cakes!

So one day he ran hooting and hollering to Grandma's little house in the hollow. Grandma could hear him coming a mile away.

"Make me some griddle cakes, Grandma, because I'm as strong and hungry as a horse," Gregory howled.

Grandma had to put her hands to her ears. "Gracious Gregory, but that was loud! Of course I'll make you griddle cakes. But before I make griddle cakes for you, isn't there something you'd like to do for me?"

It was just some little chore she had in mind.

But Gregory thought she wanted to see how strong he was. So he went hooting and hollering up Hogan's Hill where there was a honey bear looking for honey. And that honey bear was the huffiest honey bear in Grangers Grove.

Gregory hopped on the back of that honey bear and held on.

Gregory held on to that honey bear until he took him to Grandma's little house in the hollow.

And that honey bear sat in Grandma's hammock and huffed.

But a honey bear that sat in her hammock and huffed wasn't what Grandma needed. "Now Gregory," she said, "I know you're a fine, strong boy. But there's something else I want you to do."

And Grandma was going to tell him.

But Gregory was off hooting and hollering to Mr. Murphy's meadow where there was a mule that nobody could move. And that was the most mulish mule in Grangers Grove.

Gregory hopped on the back of that mule and wouldn't get off. First that mule kicked…

...and then he sat down. But Gregory got behind that mule and pushed. He pushed that sitting-down mule all the way to Grandma's little house in the hollow.

SUGA
COOK
JAM

Grandma made batter from the fresh-laid eggs and poured it into the hot pan. And when she had browned her cakes on one side, she tossed them to brown them on the other. And those griddle cakes were so fluffy they floated.

And those three little hens sat right down in the straw
and laid enough eggs to fill Grandma's big brown basket.

Grandma went to the hen yard to talk to her hens, and for the first time Gregory listened. Grandma's voice was as mild as May. Gregory watched her from the window, gentling her hens, and she was as gentle as June.

Grandma sat Gregory to dry before her stove in her little house in the hollow. And there wasn't a hoot nor a holler out of him.

They all helped to haul Gregory out of Grandma's well.

It was lucky Gregory came down in Grandma's well. Gregory landed with a splash, and that was the biggest splash in Grangers Grove.

And that mule sat on Grandma's welcome mat and moped.

But a mulish mule that sat on her welcome mat and moped wasn't what Grandma had in mind. "Now Gregory, if you'll just stop and listen! Because for griddle cakes I have to beat batter, and all I want is some eggs for my batter."

"Oh eggs, Grandma! Why didn't you tell me?"

Gregory ran roaring up Ridley's Ridge where there was an eagle's eyrie with three big eagle's eggs. And those were the biggest eggs in Grangers Grove.

At that the honey bear stopped huffing and the mulish mule stopped moping. And that bear and that mule and Grandma all waited for Gregory to come down.

And then he jumped so high you couldn't hear him holler any more.

Then Gregory was so mad, he hollered and he jumped. And then he jumped and he hollered.

Now those hens were the best layers in Grangers Grove. But Gregory's hollering scared the gray hen green, and it scared the brown hen blue, and the speckled hen came out in big spots all over.

And not one egg could they lay for Gregory.

Gregory went hooting into the hen yard. "LAY ME SOME EGGS!" he hollered at Grandma's three little hens.

Gregory put the eggs in his hat and went hooting and hollering all the way down to Grandma's little house in the hollow.

When Grandma saw those big eggs, she sighed. "Now Gregory, whatever would I do with big eagle's eggs in my batter when what I need is little eggs—little eggs fresh laid by my own three little hens."

"Oh, **little eggs**, Grandma! Is that all!"

Then the honey bear wiggled his nose and Mr. Murphy's mule twitched his muzzle, and that bear and that mule followed their noses right into Grandma's little house in the hollow.

"Sit down and eat them while they're hot," said Grandma, and she smiled at them all.

Now the honey bear ate three stacks of Grandma's griddle cakes with honey, and Mr. Murphy's mule ate three stacks with molasses. But Gregory ate three stacks with strawberry jam.

And when they were finished, the honey bear gave Grandma a big honey bear hug, and Mr. Murphy's mule gave Grandma a big molasses smile.

But Gregory gave Grandma a strawberry jam kiss. And that was the sweetest kiss Grandma ever had.